What Will I Do If I Can't Tie My Shoe?

To my great-niece Jessica
— H.K.

To Joe and Tommy
— D.R.

ISBN 0-590-96548-4

30 29   8 9 10 11 12/0

Printed in the U.S.A.   23
First printing, September 1997

What Will I Do If I Can't Tie My Shoe?

by Heidi Kilgras
Illustrated by Dana Regan

SCHOLASTIC INC.
New York   Toronto   London   Auckland   Sydney

My lace has come loose.

My shoe is untied.

I can't tie my lace.

I've tried and I've tried.

Buckles are easy.
Zippers are, too.

I can button my buttons,
but I can't tie my shoe!

I can slip on my slippers
faster than fast.

My sneakers with Velcro
go on in a flash.

But here I am,
stuck with my shoelace untied.

I can't run. I can't jump.
And I can't go outside!

If my lace
is undone,
I can't play.
It's no fun!

Hey, big brother, will you show me how it's done?

First, cross both ends.
Slip one over, under, and through.

Now, pull them tight.
Then here's what you do.

Next, make a "bunny ear"

and then make another.

Wrap one around,

pull it through.

You try, little brother.

I try and I try.
I think I can do it.

Look! It's a bow!
There was nothing to it!

I did it! I did it!
I tied my own shoe.
Add *this* to the list
of the things I can do.

Now I'm practically flying—

I can race, twirl, and skip!

With my shoelaces tied
I probably won't trip...

Oops!